LEFT FIELD BEAR

For Jan -
Bear-y Reading

story by Jean Rogers

Jean Rogers

pictures by Julianna Humphreys

Julianna Humphreys
August, 1996

LapCat Publications
Juneau, Alaska

LapCat Publications
R. M. and P. K. Davis
P.O. Box 20465
Juneau, Alaska 99802-0465

ISBN 0-9641998-2-3
LCCN 95-081527

Printed in Juneau, Alaska by
Alaska Litho

For Phyllis, Inspirer
- J. Rogers

For Juneau Little Leaguers
(who are bearish on baseball)
- J. Humphreys

A Mama bear and her cub were feasting in a garbage can at Melvin Park before the baseball game of the evening started. When the first two cars arrived Mama bear hurried her cub up a large spruce tree at the far end of the field.

"You stay right there," she said firmly, in the language bears use. "Don't you move until I come for you." Then she disappeared into the brush.

More cars drove up and people filled the bleachers.

The small black cub scooted right up his tree. He knew what a cuffing his mama would give him if he didn't do exactly what she told him. Settling himself comfortably between the limbs of the tree, the cub watched as several children ran out on the field.

A whistle blew and the groups of kids formed in circles. There were loud yells of "Yea, Fireballs, yea, Reliables," and the baseball game started.

Nelson was a newcomer on the Fireballs team. He ran right out to left field, close to the bear in his tree, but he didn't notice the little cub up there.

Steve, the coach of the Fireballs, had told Nelson he would have to work his way to the infield. So far, in the three games the Fireballs had played, Nelson had never hit the ball when it was his turn at bat. The Fireballs had lost every game. When Nelson stepped up to the plate all he could hear was, "Easy out, easy out." He hadn't caught a ball yet, either. Not much happened in left field.

This evening the Fireballs were playing the Reliables, the hottest team in the league. The Reliables won all the time. The Reliables were up to bat first. The game took quite awhile before they made their three outs but no balls came Nelson's way. The game continued that way for several innings.

The little blackie up in the tree found everything interesting. Humans did do some very strange things. There was a lot of running and shouting and chasing after a small, round object.

There were very unusual smells, too. Something tangy that made the bear cub's nose prickle and something sweet that made him lick his lips. He really wanted to climb down from the tree and investigate all this, but of course he didn't. Who knew when Mama bear would come back? So the cub stayed up the tree and watched.

Innings went by and Nelson's team was always out before he got a chance to bat. He got a lot of practice running back to left field.

It was the fifth inning before Nelson spied the small black bear in the tree. "Hey, guys, look who's watching the game," he called, but Reliable's third baseman was up at bat and no one heard him. This kid, the biggest one on Reliable's team, was a good hitter. Every Fireball and a lot of the mothers and fathers watching the game were yelling, "Move back, move back." Nelson did, half of him hoping the ball would sail his way so he could make a glorious catch, the other half hoping it would go straight to Nancy, the shortstop. Nancy would try to catch anything. Fast balls didn't scare her.

Now Nelson was closer to the cub's tree. He could see the small bear plainly. He'd read in his animal encyclopedia that bears get along with their sharp sense of smell and didn't depend on eyesight, but this bear didn't seem to know that. He was watching the scene intently.

Nelson kept one eye on the game and one eye on the little black cub. The bear was sitting on a branch fairly high up in the tree, leaning on the main trunk. He looked very much at home and he certainly had a bird's eye view of the game. Nelson was glad that no one had heard him. Suddenly he wanted this furry member of the audience to be his secret. He hoped no one else would notice.

Brad, the big hitter, made it to third base. The ball didn't come anywhere near Nelson before it was his team's turn at bat again. Nelson didn't get up to bat that time either.

Back out in the field, the bear was still sitting and watching. "Hi, I'm back," Nelson called softly. The bear seemed to hear him and looked down with a very friendly look.

It wasn't until the sixth inning that some small boys and girls, tired of sitting in the stands, ran out behind the ball field. They were warned to stay behind the fencing at the other end of the park, but no one paid too much attention. Even big Brad wasn't likely to send a ball that far.

When these small children spied the little bear, they set up such a hullabaloo that the game came to a standstill while everyone rushed to have a look. Several youngsters began heaving rocks and sticks up toward the bear. This made the bear nervous and he climbed farther up the tree, getting perilously near the top where the branches were too small to hold even a little bear.

"Stop that, stop!" Nelson yelled with all his might. "Leave him alone. He's just watching the game. He's not hurting anything."

A police car drove up to the edge of the field. The policeman came over to the crowd. "All right, what's going on here?"

Nelson looked at the gun on the policeman's hip. It looked big and black and terrible. Was he going to shoot the bear? The thought made Nelson's stomach churn.

Up in the tree the branches were trembling and shaking beneath the weight of the little bear. Suddenly he looked very, very small.

Nelson's legs were wobbling with fear, but he went over to the policeman. "The bear is only watching the game," he said. "He's not doing anything bad."

The officer smiled down at Nelson, then looked back up the tree. "All right," he shouted. "Get back to your ball game, folks. If you don't bother this little fella up there, he's not going to bother you. Go on now," he said to the small children as the grown-ups began moving back to the bleachers. "He paid for a good seat. Let's just let him watch the rest of the game in peace."

The policeman went back to his car to watch for any Mama bear who might come to see how her baby bear was doing.

The game went on and Nelson finally got to bat. Even from home base he could see that his bear was watching him closely. Usually it made Nelson very uncomfortable to know that anyone was watching him. Now he forgot all about his mother and father and everyone else in the stands. His only thought was to hit the ball and make it go anyplace but left field. The police car was still there so his bear was safe in his tree. Nelson wanted it to stay that way.

Smack! His bat connected hard with the ball. For a second Nelson was so surprised he forgot to drop the bat and run. But then he made it safely to third base. The cub was still watching him. Nelson had time to give him a wave before the next Fireball sent the ball flying. When Nelson crossed home plate, the cheers and yells were the sweetest sounds he thought he had ever heard.

"By Golly", said Steve, the coach, thumping Nelson on the back so hard it nearly knocked him off his feet. "That's the way to play ball." Nelson had made the first score. "It's a milkshake for everyone if we win," Steve shouted as another Fireball runner crossed the plate. The Fireballs had finally caught fire.

After the game, as he slurped his chocolate shake happily, Nelson wished he could share his drink with the bear. "If bears like honey," Nelson thought, "they would surely go for this chocolate ice cream." The Fireballs couldn't stop talking about their wonderful victory.

"Boy," Obie said, tipping his milkshake up and licking up the last dribbles, "Nelson, you sure changed our luck today." There were a lot of yells of agreement and "Yea, Nelson."

That was music for Nelson's ears, but to himself he said, "Thanks, little bear, you were a good luck mascot."

Back at the ball park everyone had driven away. The police car went last of all. The cub was still perched in the topmost branches of his tree. When the Alaska twilight finally deepened into near darkness, Mama bear came back to collect her baby.

Who knows what that cub told Mama about that game in the language bears use. There was such a lot to tell. And he had seen everything there was to see, that little bear. After all he had the very best seat in the house!